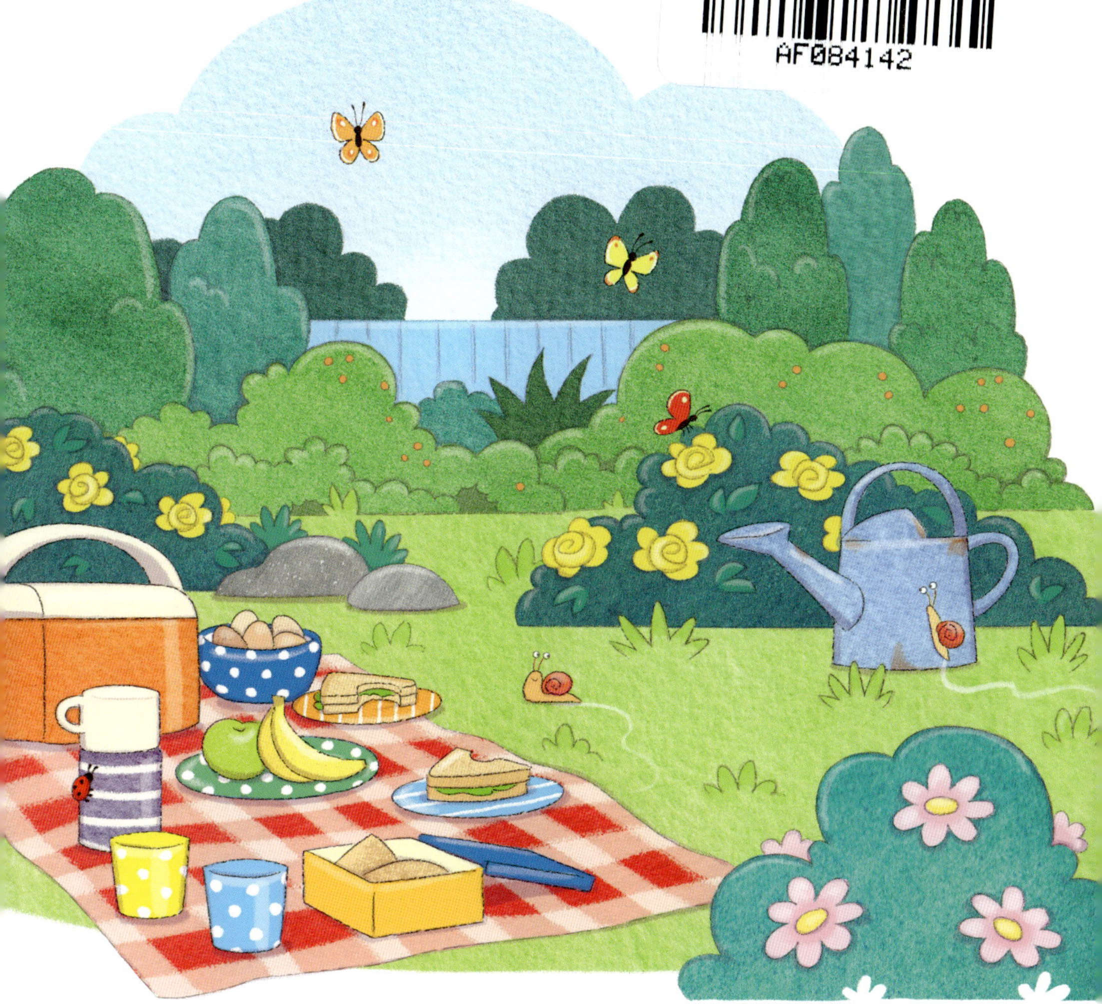

Peek-a-boo!

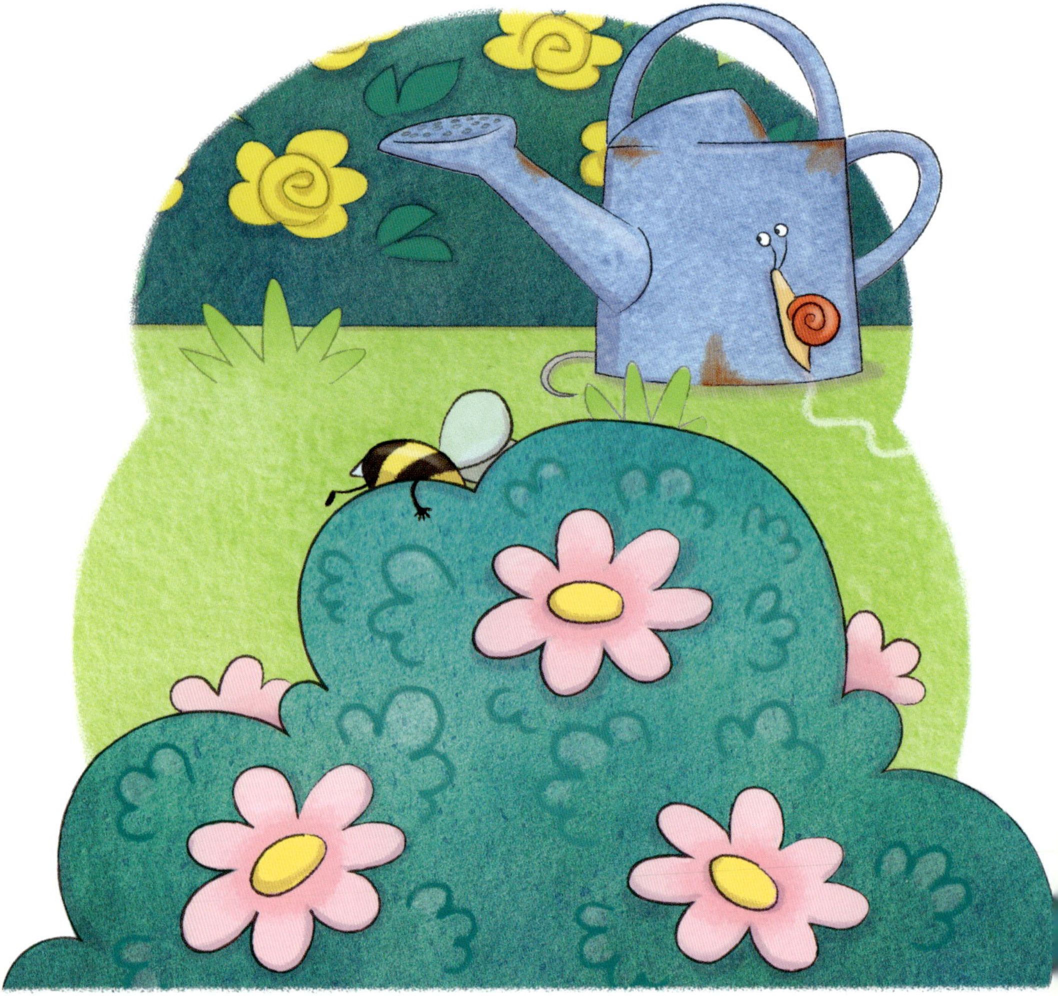

A leg, a wing...

I can see... Bee!

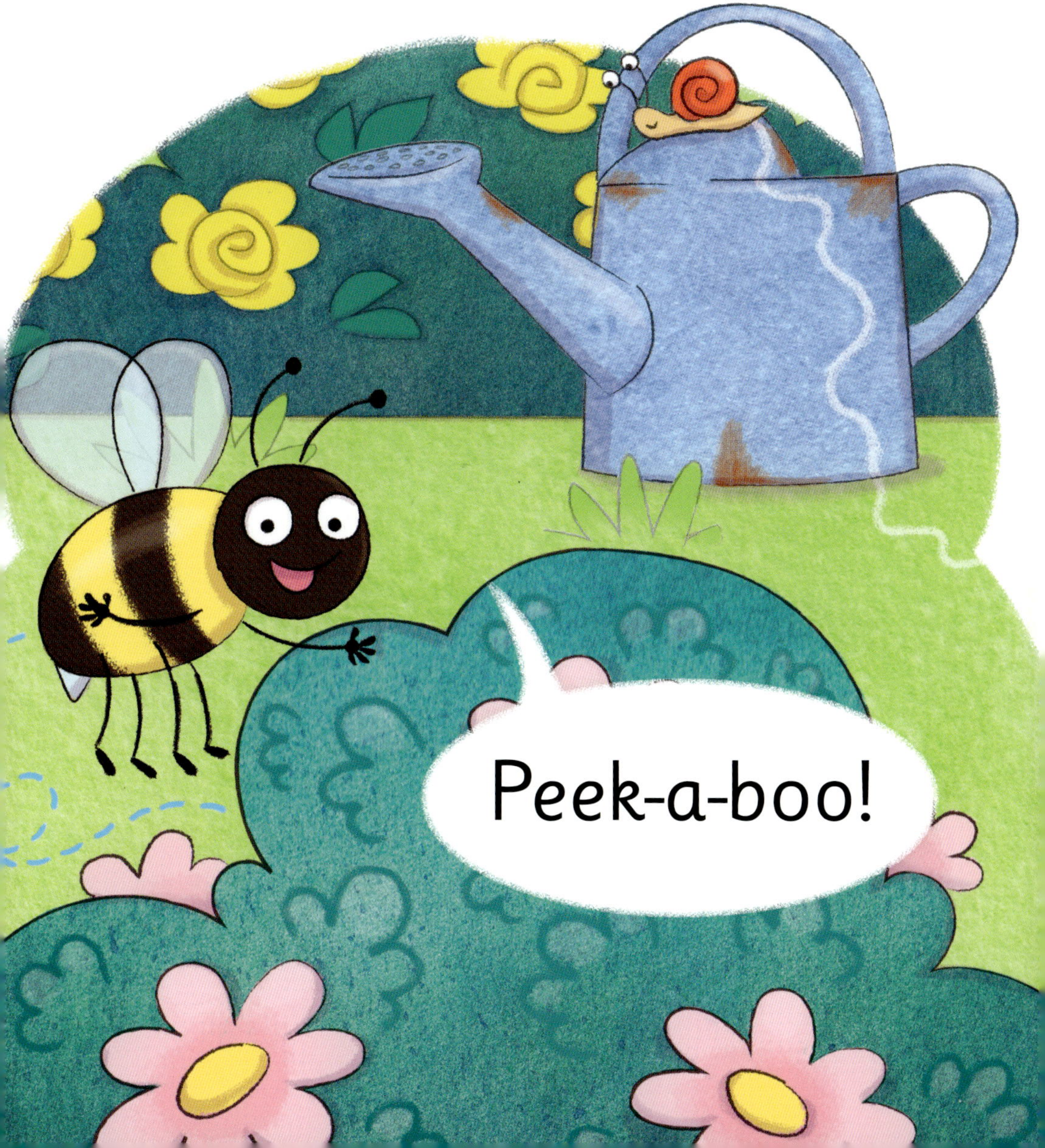

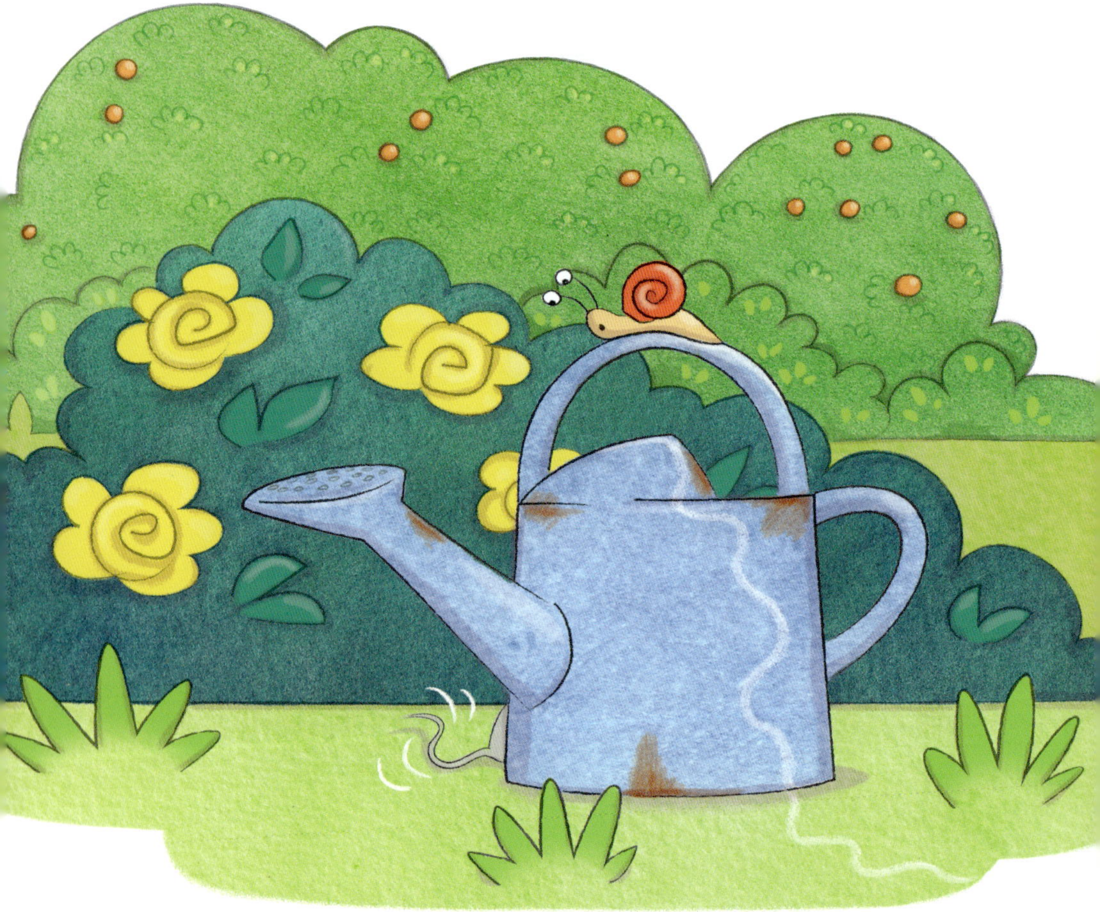

A long, thin tail...

I can see... a mouse!

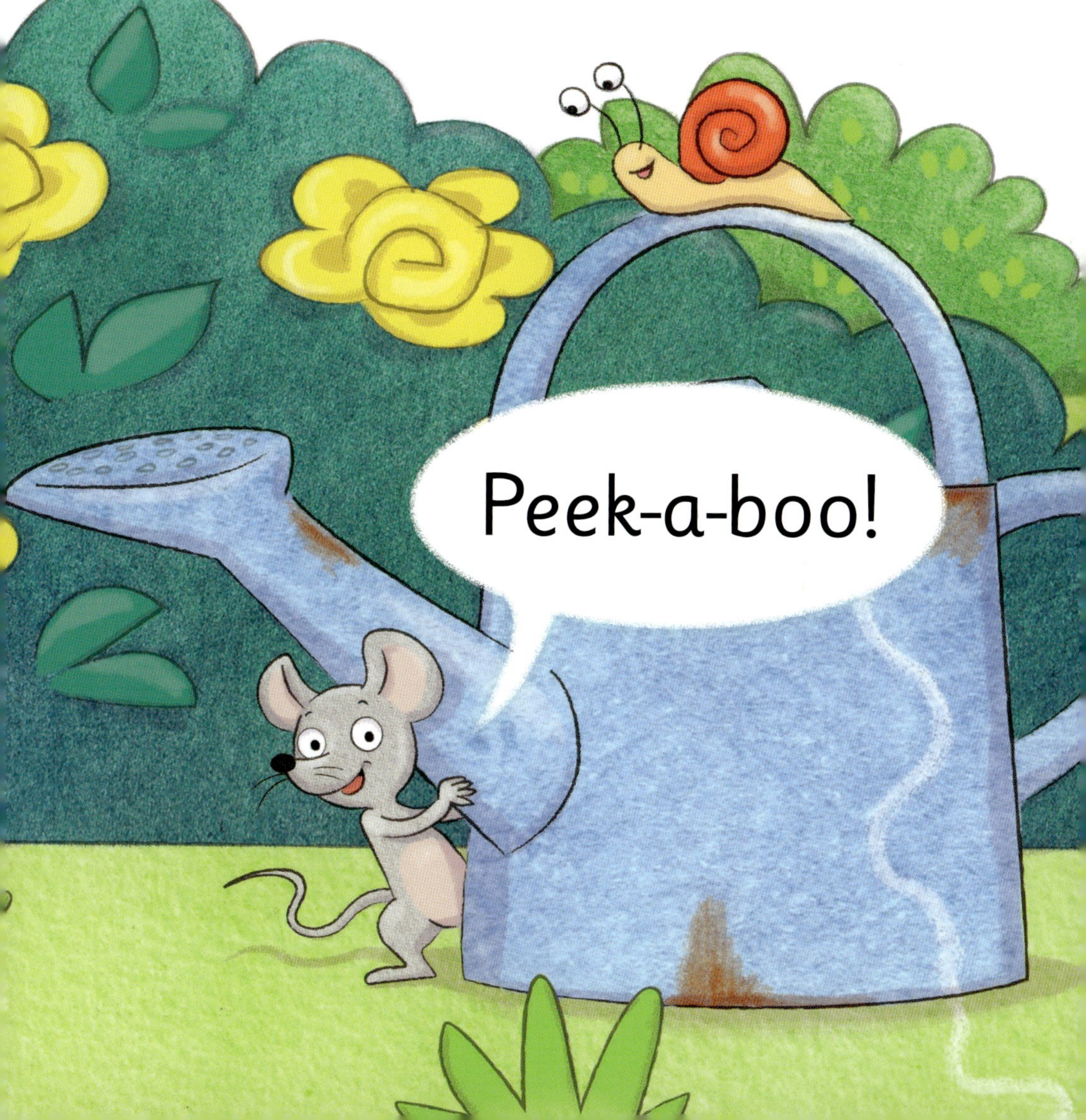

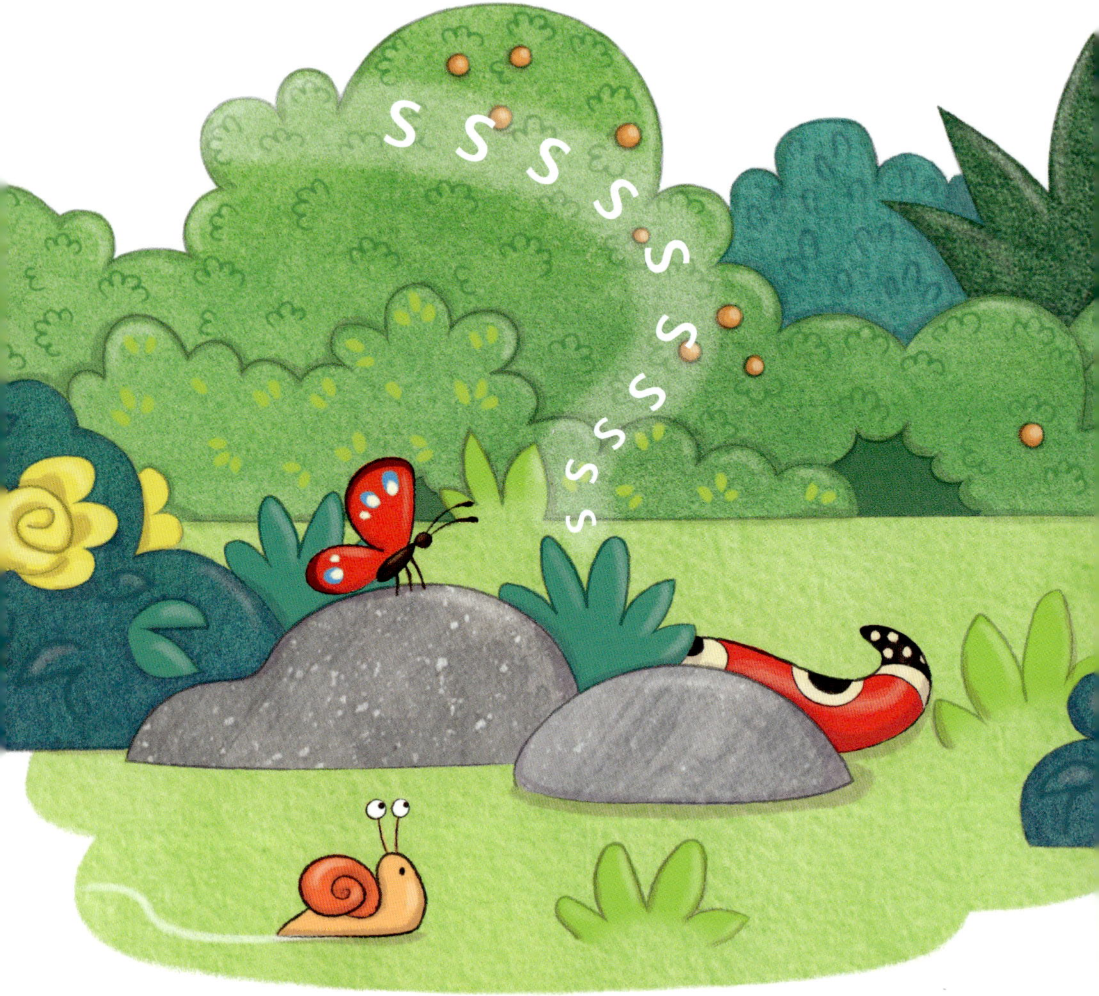

A red tail with spots...

I can see...

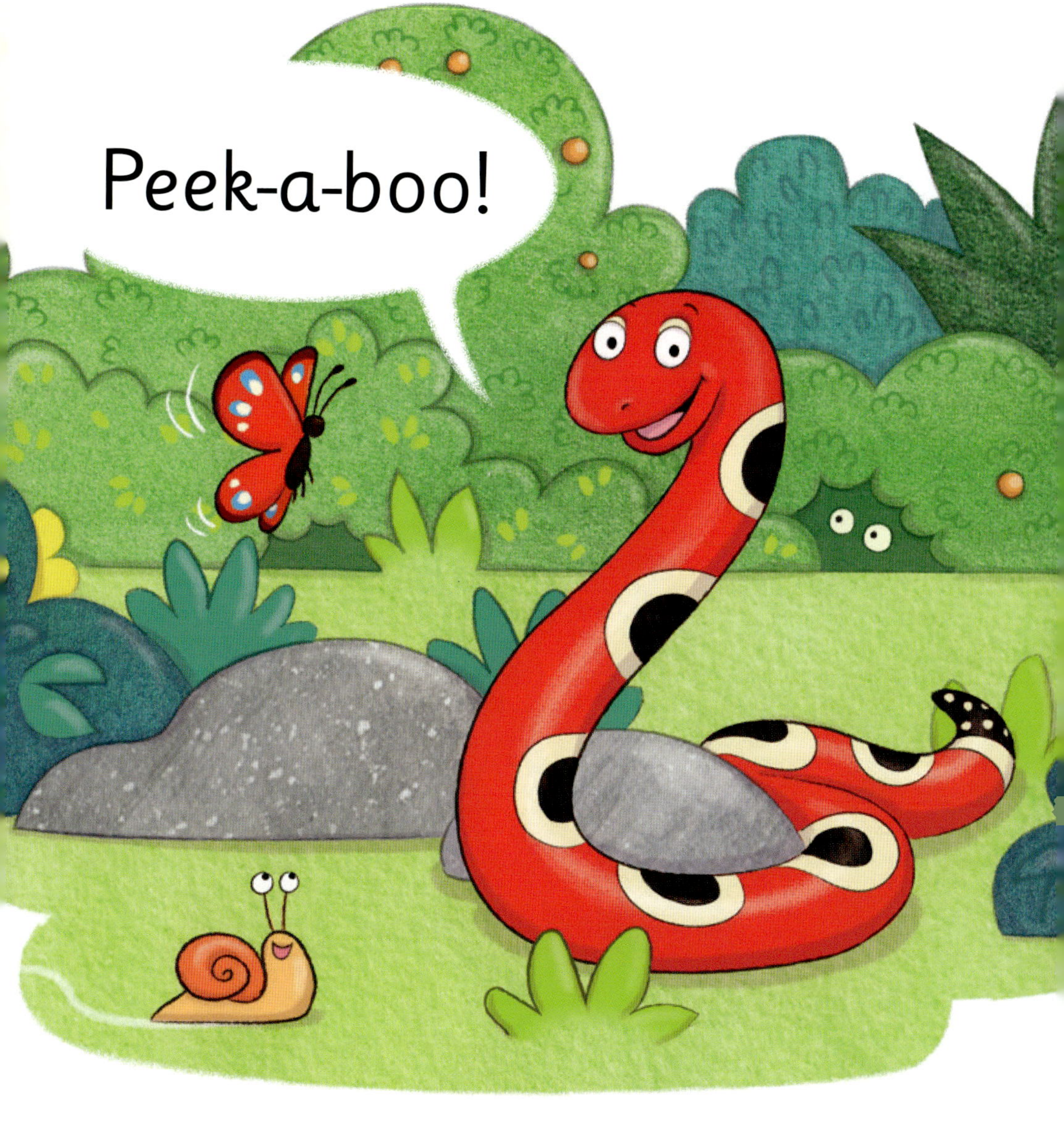

Peek-a-boo is fun.

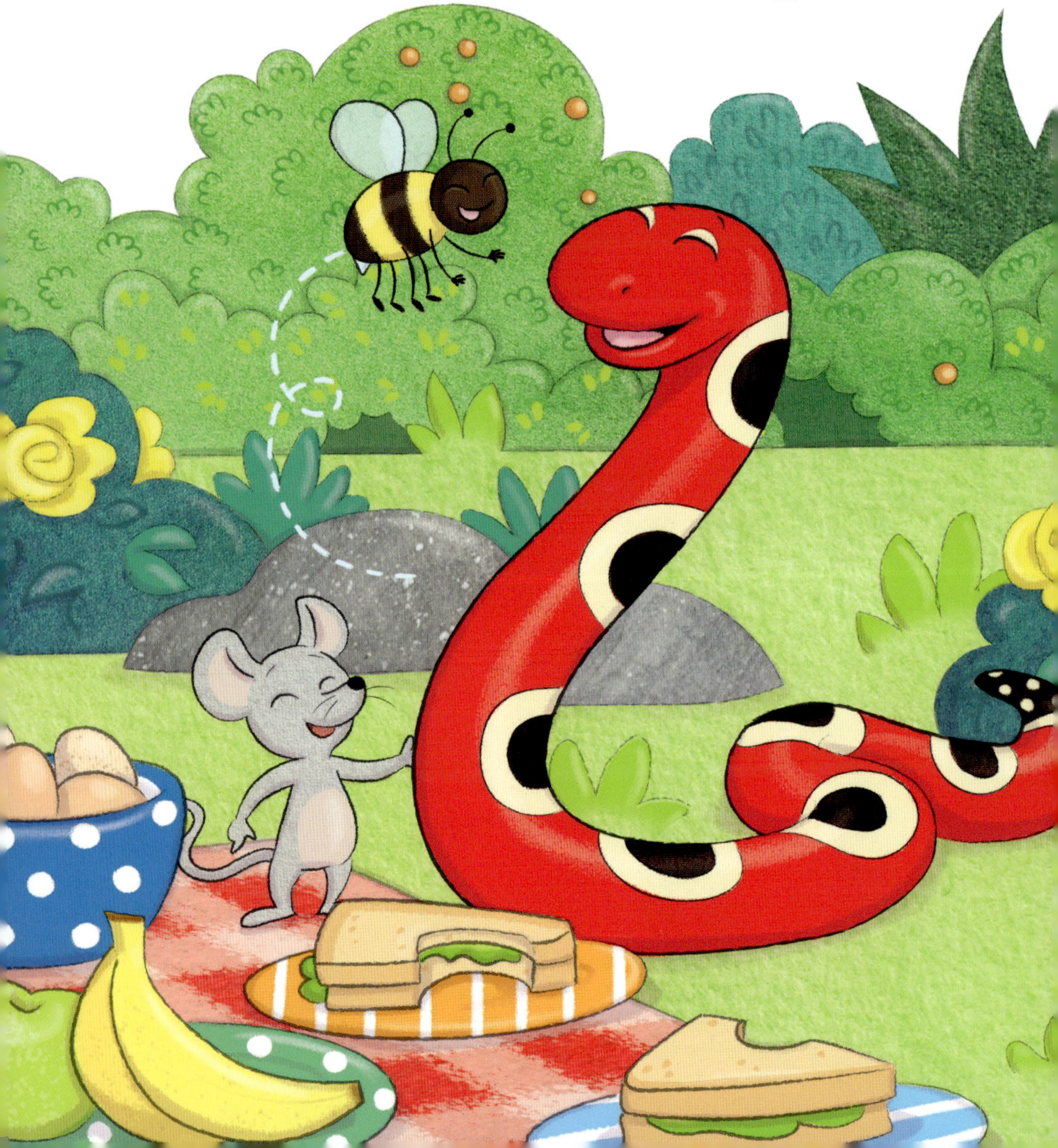